LiON IS NERVOUS

A book about feeling WORRiED

Written by Sue Graves

Illustrated by Trevor Dunton

Franklin Watts®
An imprint of Scholastic Inc.

Lion was always worrying. He worried about **everything**! He worried if he was late for school.

He worried if he was early, too.

Lion even worried about getting all his math problems right . . . and he was really good at math. Lion always got nervous when he worried. He felt hot and dizzy. His tummy fluttered and his knees knocked. It was a **horrible** feeling.

On Friday, Miss Bird had some exciting news. She said the class was going on a **field trip** in two weeks. She said this year they were all going to Adventure Land and Mr. Croc was going to take them on the school bus. Everyone clapped and cheered. Adventure Land was the best amusement park! **Everyone was excited**. Everyone, that is, except Lion—he began to worry.

All during soccer practice, Lion worried about the field trip. He worried about getting to Adventure Land. What if the school bus **broke down**? What if they couldn't get to Adventure Land at all? That would be **awful**! Lion got so nervous that he let in lots of goals.

On Monday, Lion worried that it might **rain** on the day of the field trip. That would be no fun at all. And what if it rained so hard that Adventure Land flooded and had to close? That would be **terrible**! Lion got so nervous that he knocked paint all over Hippo's picture.

Monkey and Hippo were worried about Lion.
They asked him if he was all right. But Lion did
not tell them he was worried about the field trip.
He was afraid they would laugh at him.

The next day, Lion worried about **the rides** at Adventure Land. What if he was too small to go on them . . . or too big? That would be **awful**! Lion got so nervous that he knocked all the pencils and books onto the floor. Miss Bird took Lion outside to **calm down**.

Miss Bird asked Lion what was wrong. He told her all his worries about the field trip. Miss Bird listened carefully. She said that when she felt worried she took a **deep breath**. Lion took a deep breath. He felt a **little better**.

Then Miss Bird told him to think about all the **good things** that might happen on the field trip, instead of all the bad things. Lion thought about it.

He thought about the school bus. Mr. Croc
took good care of it. He always checked the
tires. He always checked the oil. The school
bus might not break down at all. Lion felt
much better.

Then he thought about the weather. There were no clouds in the sky, and it hadn't rained for weeks and weeks. It might not rain at all on the day of the field trip. Adventure Land might not flood and then it would stay open **all day**! Lion felt a **lot better**.

Then Miss Bird told Lion that everyone gets worried sometimes. She said Lion could always talk about his worries with his friends. Lion said that Monkey and Hippo were his **best** friends. Miss Bird said they would be very good friends to talk to if he felt worried again. Lion felt **much, much better**.

On Friday, it was time for the field trip.
The school bus did not break down at all.

And it only rained in the afternoon when everyone was on the water ride, so it **didn't matter** anyway.

Lion was a bit too big to go on the Runaway Train, but he **didn't mind** at all. He went on the Roaring Rocket instead, and that was **even more fun**!

Then Miss Bird looked at her watch. She said there was just enough time for everyone to go on **the Big Drop**. The Big Drop was the highest, fastest, and scariest ride in Adventure Land.

Everyone was very excited. But Lion began to worry. What if the ride was too high and too fast? What if it was **too scary**? Even worse, what if he could not sit next to his friends? That would be **really horrible**!

Then Lion remembered what Miss Bird had told him. He took a **deep breath**. He felt a little better. He told Monkey and Hippo his worries. Monkey said the ride could not be too high, too fast, or too scary because everyone was having **lots** of fun on it. Then Hippo said that they would all sit together so that Lion felt safe. Lion felt **much better**.

The Big Drop was very high and very fast . . . and it was **very scary**! Lion felt hot and dizzy. His tummy fluttered and his knees knocked. But Lion wasn't worried. He wasn't worried at all. He was having a **great** time!

A note about sharing this book

The **Behavior Matters** series has been developed to provide a starting point for further discussion on children's behavior both in relation to themselves and others. The series features animal characters reflecting typical behavior traits often seen in young children.

Lion Is Nervous

This story explores some of the typical worries experienced by children. The book aims to encourage children to develop strategies for dealing with anxiety. It also looks at ways in which others might help someone overcome their concerns.

How to use the book

The book is designed for adults to share with either an individual child or a group of children, and as a starting point for discussion.

The book also provides visual support and repeated words and phrases to build reading confidence.

Before reading the story

Choose a time to read when you and the children are relaxed and have time to share the story.

Spend time looking at the illustrations and talk about what the book might be about before reading it together.

Encourage children to tackle new words by sounding them out.

After reading, talk about the book with the children:

- Encourage the children to retell the events of the story in chronological order.

- Talk about Lion's worries. Ask the children if they worry about similar things. Invite them to share their worries with the others. Take the opportunity to point out that many people worry about the same things.

- Ask the children to explain how they feel when they get worried. Do they get butterflies in their tummies when faced with something new or different? Do they feel shaky and uncertain? Ask them how they handle these feelings. Have any of the children developed their own strategies for dealing with these physical features of anxiety?

- As a group, ask the children to take a deep breath and exhale slowly. Ask them how this makes them feel. Do they feel calmer? Point out that this is a good strategy for dealing with anxiety.

- Extend this by talking about other ways children can calm themselves or others who feel anxious. Who would the children confide in? Would they prefer to share their worries with friends, parents, or caregivers? Why?

- Place the children into groups of three or four. Ask them to find one particular worry that they all share, e.g. worrying about school work, worrying about friendships, etc. Ask each group to discuss how they could overcome their concerns.

- Invite the groups to return and ask a spokesperson from each group to talk about their findings. Encourage the others to comment on the concerns raised and the resolutions suggested.

Library of Congress Cataloging-in-Publication Data
Names: Graves, Sue, 1950– author. | Dunton, Trevor, illustrator.
Title: Lion is nervous: a book about feeling worried/written by Sue Graves; illustrated
   by Trevor Dunton.
Description: First edition. | New York: Franklin Watts, an imprint of Scholastic Inc., 2021. |
   Series: Behavior matters | Audience: Ages 4–7. | Audience: Grades K–1. | Summary: The
   class field trip is coming up, and Lion worries about the weather, the rides, and everything else—
   and his anxiety makes him clumsy which causes his friends to worry about him.
Identifiers: LCCN 2021000565 (print) | LCCN 2021000566 (ebook) | ISBN 9781338758177
   (library binding) | ISBN 9781338758184 (paperback) | ISBN 9781338758191 (ebook)
Subjects: LCSH: Worry—Juvenile fiction. | Anxiety—Juvenile fiction. | Lion—Juvenile fiction. |
   School field trips—Juvenile fiction. | CYAC: Worry—Fiction. | Anxiety—Fiction. | Lion—
   Fiction. | School field trips—Fiction.
Classification: LCC PZ7.G7754 Li 2021 (print) | LCC PZ7.G7754 (ebook) |
   DDC 823.914 [E]—dc23
LC record available at https://lccn.loc.gov/2021000565
LC ebook record available at https://lccn.loc.gov/2021000566

10 9 8 7 6 5 4 3 2 1   22 23 24 25 26 27

Printed in China
First edition, 2022